**Put Beginning Readers on the Right Track with
ALL ABOARD READING™**

The All Aboard Reading series is especially designed for beginning readers. Written by noted authors and illustrated in full color, these are books that children really want to read—books to excite their imagination, expand their interests, make them laugh, and support their feelings. With fiction and nonfiction stories that are high interest and curriculum-related, All Aboard Reading books offer something for every young reader. And with four different reading levels, the All Aboard Reading series lets you choose which books are most appropriate for your children and their growing abilities.

Picture Readers
Picture Readers have super-simple texts, with many nouns appearing as rebus pictures. At the end of each book are 24 flash cards—on one side is a rebus picture; on the other side is the written-out word.

Station Stop 1
Station Stop 1 books are best for children who have just begun to read. Simple words and big type make these early reading experiences more comfortable. Picture clues help children to figure out the words on the page. Lots of repetition throughout the text helps children to predict the next word or phrase—an essential step in developing word recognition.

Station Stop 2
Station Stop 2 books are written specifically for children who are reading with help. Short sentences make it easier for early readers to understand what they are reading. Simple plots and simple dialogue help children with reading comprehension.

Station Stop 3
Station Stop 3 books are perfect for children who are reading alone. With longer text and harder words, these books appeal to children who have mastered basic reading skills. More complex stories captivate children who are ready for more challenging books.

In addition to All Aboard Reading books, look for All Aboard Math Readers™ (fiction stories that teach math concepts children are learning in school) and All Aboard Science Readers™ (nonfiction books that explore the most fascinating science topics in age-appropriate language).

All Aboard for happy reading!

For Alison, with
heart and sole—S.H.

For everyone who tries and tries:
don't give up! You can do it!—A.W.

Library of Congress Cataloging-in-Publication Data

Hood, Susan.
   Look! I can tie my shoes / by Susan Hood ; illustrated by Amy Wummer.
       p. cm. — (All aboard reading) "Level 1."
    Summary: A young girl loves all kinds of shoes except the ones with laces, until her mother
gives her—and the reader—a lesson in tying shoes.
   [1. Shoes—Fiction. 2. Stories in rhyme.] I. Wummer, Amy, ill. II. Title. III. Series.
   PZ8.3.H7577 Lr   2002
   [E]—dc21

                                       2002004030

ISBN 0-448-42676-5   I J

Station Stop 1

LOOK!
I Can Tie My Shoes!

By Susan Hood
Illustrated by Amy Wummer

Grosset & Dunlap • New York

I love shoes!

I love high-tops.

I love flip-flops.

I love jellies.

I love wellies!

Shoes with bows

or cutout toes.

Funny flippers . . .

and bunny slippers!

Yes, I love shoes!

But not these shoes!

Mom asks me why.
"I cannot tie . . ."

"You can do it.

There's nothing to it."

Mom says,

"I'll show you how.

Right here, right now."

Tie a loop.

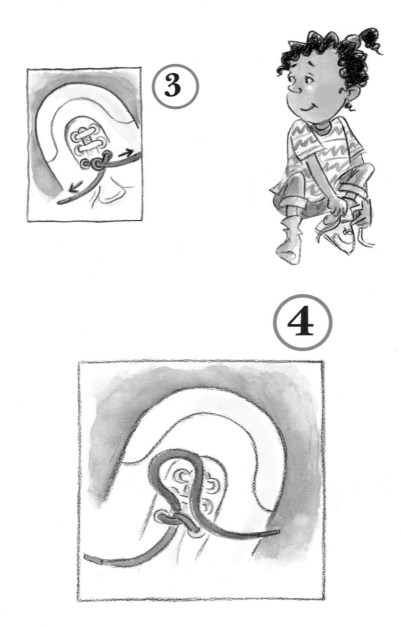

Then wrap like this.

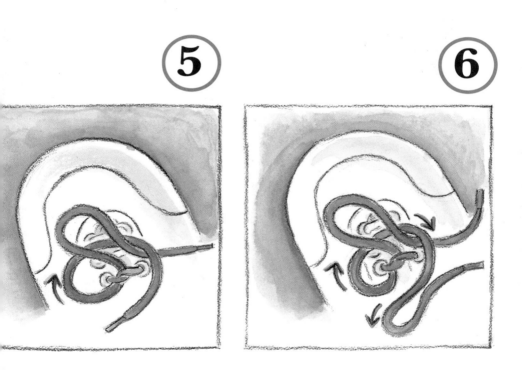

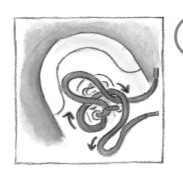

Go under.

Pull.

Oops! I missed!

I try and try
to learn to tie!

Loop a loop.

Wrap like this.

Go under.

Pull.

Hug and kiss!

I can do it!

Nothing to it!